CLASSIC STARTS™

The Adventures of Sherlock Holmes

*Retold from the Sir Arthur Conan Doyle
original by Chris Sasaki*

Illustrated by Lucy Corvino

STERLING CHILDREN'S BOOKS
New York

STERLING CHILDREN'S BOOKS
New York

An Imprint of Sterling Publishing
387 Park Avenue South
New York, NY 10016

Text © 2005 by Chris Sasaki
Illustrations © 2005 by Lucy Corvino

ISBN 978-1-4027-9461-2

Distributed in Canada by Sterling Publishing
c/o Canadian Manda Group, 165 Dufferin Street
Toronto, Ontario, Canada M6K 3H6
Distributed in the United Kingdom by GMC Distribution Services
Castle Place, 166 High Street, Lewes, East Sussex, England BN7 1XU
Distributed in Australia by Capricorn Link (Australia) Pty. Ltd.
P.O. Box 704, Windsor, NSW 2756, Australia

Classic Starts is a trademark of Sterling Publishing Co., Inc.

For information about custom editions, special sales, and premium and corporate purchases, please contact Sterling
Special Sales at 800-805-5489 or specialsales@sterlingpublishing.com.

Printed in China
Lot #:
2 4 6 8 10 9 7 5 3
04/12

www.sterlingpublishing.com/kids

CONTENTS

A Scandal in Bohemia

⌒

To Sherlock Holmes, she is always *the* woman—the woman who outsmarted him. All my friend has to say is "the woman," and I know who he is talking about. Her name was Irene Adler.

Let me introduce myself: My name is Dr. Watson. Holmes and I shared rooms together on 221B Baker Street until I got married. We lived there as friends for years, with me helping him in his investigations. Later I turned many of those adventures into stories for my readers.

One night, I was walking about London when

I found myself on Baker Street. It was March 20, 1888. I looked up and saw Holmes in the second-floor window. I could see his tall, lean figure pacing back and forth. His head was lowered, but I could still see his hawk-like nose and strong chin. He held his hands behind his back. My old friend was hard at work. I hadn't seen him for a long time, so I rang the bell and went in.

Holmes looked at me with his sharp, keen eyes and greeted me with a smile. He seemed relaxed, with his long, bony body stretched out on his favorite old sofa. I found myself at ease again as I breathed in the musty air of his parlor, where we had gone over the details of so many cases together. Then he spoke. "I see you are enjoying marriage, Watson," he said. "I would say you've gained seven and a half pounds since I saw you last. I also see that you have returned to your practice as a medical doctor. I'm sorry you were caught in the rain recently. And equally sorry

that you have a careless servant at home."

"My dear Holmes," I said with surprise, "I *have* put on seven pounds since I saw you last. And I was caught in a downpour in the country last Thursday. You are correct in thinking my wife and I are not pleased with the hired help at home. But how on earth did you know?"

"Really? I was sure it was seven and a half," laughed Holmes. "It's simple, Watson. Your shoes reveal they were covered in mud recently. And I can see the scrape marks carelessly left by the person who cleaned those shoes.

"I also detect the faint smell of antiseptic on you, some sort of black powder on your finger that can only be used to treat infections. And there is a bulge in your coat where you normally carry your stethoscope. These clues tell me you are once again a man of medicine."

"It always sounds so simple when you explain it, Holmes," I said. "Yet I never understand how you get from point A to point B, though I see everything that you see."

"You see, but you do not observe," Holmes said, handing me a sheet of thick paper. "For example, what do you see in this note? Read it aloud, my friend."

"'A tall, masked man will call upon you tonight,'" I began, "'who wishes to speak to you. You have helped royal persons in the past, so I know I can trust you. This from many reliable sources have we heard.'"

"What do you make of the note, Watson?" Holmes asked.

"It is expensive paper," I replied. "Whoever sent the note is not poor." I held the paper up to the light. "Also, there are marks on the paper."

"The marks reveal much," said Holmes. "They tell me the name of the company that manufactured this particular sheet. I found out that it is located in the kingdom of Bohemia.

"That's not all," he continued. "The person who wrote this note is German. Did you notice the odd sentence, 'This from many reliable sources have we heard'? Someone who spoke French or Russian would not have written a sentence like that. It could only be written by a German-speaking person. And, if I am not mistaken, here he comes now . . ."

From outside came the sound of horses' hooves and carriage wheels. Moments later, someone rang the bell. This was followed by the soft thud of footsteps on the stairs and a loud knock on the door.

A very large man entered the parlor. He was over six feet tall and very muscular. He wore a fancy coat and a deep blue cape. The cape was fastened at his neck with a large gemstone. Our visitor's boots were high and topped off with fur. He held a large hat in one hand. With his other, he adjusted an eye mask that covered the upper part of his face.

"Please, sit down," said Holmes. "This is my friend and colleague, Dr. Watson. Anything you say to me, you may say to my trusted companion."

"Mr. Holmes," said the stranger, "I am Count Von Kramm. I am a Bohemian nobleman. I need to speak to you about a matter of extreme importance. And I prefer to speak to you alone."

I got up to leave, but Holmes grabbed my arm. "If you will not speak to both of us, then I cannot help you."

"Very well," answered our visitor. "But I must begin by asking you both to keep these matters secret for two years. After that, it will not matter. But for now, the fate of Europe depends upon your silence."

Holmes and I promised to keep the matter

secret. Our visitor continued. "Please forgive the mask. The person who sent me must keep his name unknown. I haven't even given you my real name."

"I know," said Holmes.

The masked man continued. "These events could create a terrible scandal for the royal family of Bohemia."

"I know that also," added Holmes. "Please, Your Majesty, continue."

Our guest suddenly became upset and paced the room nervously. Then he grabbed the mask, tore it from his face, and threw it to the floor. "You're correct, Mr. Holmes!" he cried. "I can hide nothing from you. I haven't been sent by a member of the royal family. I *am* the King! I am Wilhelm Gottsreich Sigismond von Ormstein, Grand Duke of Cassel-Felstein, King of Bohemia. My problem is so serious that I could not risk sending another in my place. I trust only myself to tell you my story!"

"Then, please," said Holmes, "tell me."

"It all began five years ago. I was visiting Warsaw, Poland, and met a woman named Irene Adler. Perhaps you know of her."

"Please, Doctor," Holmes said to me, "what does the 'Index' have to say about Miss Adler?"

Holmes kept a large book filled with every sort of newspaper clipping and bit of information he could find. He called the book the "Index." I took the "Index" from the shelf, found the name "Irene Adler," and handed it to Holmes.

"Let me see," he said. "Born in Liverpool in 1858. An opera singer, I see. Sang with the Imperial Opera of Warsaw. Retired from singing and living in London." He looked up at the King. "And so, you fell in love with this woman in Warsaw."

"That's correct, Mr. Holmes," said our royal visitor. "But now I am to be married to another—a Norwegian princess. If her family were to find out about Miss Adler, it would ruin everything! But that is the problem. Miss Adler does not want me to marry. She threatens to send our love letters to my fiancée."

"You could say the letters were forged," offered Holmes.

"She has a framed photograph of the two of us together," said the King.

"Oh, dear. That is a problem," said Holmes. "You must get it back, even if you have to steal it or buy it."

The King replied. "I tried to get it back, Mr. Holmes. My men broke into her house. But they couldn't find it. And she won't take any amount of money for it. She says she is going to send the photograph and the letters on the day my fiancée and I announce our engagement. That will be in three days."

"Then we must get to work," said Holmes. "I will need the name of your hotel and Miss Adler's address."

"I am at the Langham Hotel under the name of Count Von Kramm," said the King, "and Miss Adler is at Briony Lodge, on Serpentine Avenue."

"Very well," said Holmes. "I will contact you at your hotel when I have news. And Watson, be so good as to call on me tomorrow at 3 P.M. I would appreciate your help in this matter."

I was at Baker Street at three the next afternoon, but Holmes was not. I had been waiting for about an hour when the street-level door opened. A man entered, dressed in dirty, ragged clothes. His chin was covered by a scraggly beard, and he walked with a limp.

It was Sherlock Holmes. I knew my friend was

a master of disguise, but it was still hard to recognize him. Holmes went into the bedroom and returned looking like himself again. He sat down by the fire and laughed.

"What a morning I've had, Watson," he said. "As you can guess from my disguise, I visited Miss Adler's house in order to watch her. There was nothing unusual about Briony Lodge. But I did observe a large sitting room on the main floor, with very large windows.

"I also spoke with several individuals on the street," he said. "I learned that Miss Adler goes out every day at five and returns home at seven. Also, there is a handsome gentleman who often visits. His name is Godfrey Norton. It seems Mr. Norton is a lawyer. Does this mean he is working for Miss Adler? Are they friends? What is their relationship? If he is working for her, perhaps he has the photograph.

"It wasn't long before a horse-drawn cab

arrived at Briony Lodge," continued Holmes. "It was Mr. Norton. He rushed from the cab and into the house. Next, I saw him pacing up and down in the sitting room. I did not see Miss Adler, but I am guessing she was with him.

"After a half hour, he emerged from the house in a great rush. Before he got back in his cab, I heard him tell the driver to hurry to the Church of St. Monica. Then they were gone.

"I was wondering what to do next, when another horse-drawn carriage pulled up. It was Miss Adler's turn to rush from the house. I only caught a brief glimpse of her, Watson, but she is a lovely woman. I can understand why the King followed his heart and not his brain.

"Miss Adler climbed into the carriage and told the driver to rush to the same church. I hailed a cab and followed. By the time I reached St. Monica, they were already there. I entered quietly and saw the couple at the front of the church.

They were with the minister. I tried to get closer, pretending that I had just wandered in off the street.

"To my great surprise, Godfrey Norton ran to me and dragged me to the altar. He said they needed a witness to make the wedding legal. And before I knew it, I had helped the couple become newlyweds!

"They thanked me and handed me some coins. I heard Miss Adler tell her new husband that she would return home at seven as usual. Then they left the church in different carriages."

"What a morning indeed, Holmes!" I said. "But now what?"

"Now, Watson," he answered, "I need your help. We must be at Briony Lodge at seven this evening when Miss Adler—or should I say, Mrs. Norton—returns home. I have already made arrangements for others to help us there. I will enter the house. Someone will then open the window to the sitting room. When I signal to you from inside, you must throw this through the window."

Holmes handed me a small tube and explained that it was a smoke bomb.

"Then," he continued, "you will yell 'Fire' as loudly as you can. Others will join you in raising the alarm. Finally, you will wait for me at the end of the street."

"You can rely on me, Holmes," I said.

My companion and I had a quiet lunch. Then Holmes disappeared into his bedroom. When he returned, he was in disguise again. This time he was dressed as a minister, in a black hat and baggy pants. But it was his manner and expression that had changed the most. I had always thought Holmes would make a great actor—here was proof.

We left Baker Street and were at Briony Lodge before seven. To my surprise, there were many people on the street. There was a group of poorly dressed men standing on the corner. Two gentlemen were talking with a young woman. Several other people walked up and down the street.

"Now that the couple are married," said Holmes, "the photograph is even more important. The king does not want his fiancée to see it. But I'm sure that Irene Adler would not want Mr. Norton to see it, either.

"But the question remains—where is the photograph? It is not small enough for her to carry it with her. She could have given it to her banker or lawyer. But I don't think she did. It's too valuable to entrust to anyone else. She would also want to put her hands on it at a moment's notice. So, it must be in the house."

"But the King's men already searched the house," I said.

"They didn't know where to look," replied Holmes.

"Then how will your search be any different?" I asked.

"I won't look for it. I'll get the woman to show me where it is."

"But why on earth would she do that, Holmes?" I asked.

Suddenly, Irene Adler's carriage pulled up in front of the house. As she was getting out, two men rushed to hold the carriage door open for her. They began to push and argue. Others joined in and soon, the woman was in the middle of a fight. In disguise, Holmes rushed to help her. But as he reached her, he gave a cry and fell to the ground. He lay motionless, blood running from his face. The men who had been fighting ran off down the street.

Irene Adler rushed past the crowd. Then, just as she was about to disappear inside, she turned and asked, "Is the poor gentleman all right?"

"I'm afraid not," said one of the crowd. "It's a

shame. He saved you from having your purse and watch stolen by that gang. Can you take him in so he can rest?"

"Of course," replied the lady. "Bring him into the sitting room and lay him on the sofa."

I stood outside and watched as Holmes was carried into the sitting room. After a minute, I saw him sit up and motion toward the window. A maid opened it and left the room. A moment later, Holmes signaled. I quickly threw the smoke bomb into the house and yelled "Fire!" Within seconds, people around me were crying out the same word. Clouds of smoke poured from the room. Then I heard Holmes' voice call out above the noise: "False alarm!"

Turning the corner, I was soon joined by my friend. "Do you have the photograph?" I asked.

"No," Holmes replied as we slowly made our way home, "but I know where it is. As expected, she showed me exactly where it is hidden.

"Let me explain, Watson. By now, you know that the people on the street were helping us. I had told them to start a fight when the lady returned home. I pretended to fall and, with the help of some red paint, I faked an injury.

"I suspected that the photograph was in the sitting room," he said. "I also knew what would happen when she heard the cry of 'Fire.' She would try to rescue her most valued possession— the photograph.

"So, as the room filled with smoke, she rushed to a hidden panel in one of the walls. She opened the panel and pulled out the photograph. When I called out the false alarm, she returned the photograph to its hiding place. At the same time, I noticed that she caught a glimpse of the smoke bomb. After that, she disappeared. I would have taken the photograph then and there, but a servant came into the room and I had to make my escape."

"Brilliant, Holmes," I said as we turned onto Baker Street. "But now what?"

"I will send a message to the King and tell him what we found," he answered. "I will ask him to join us tomorrow morning. Then we will call at Briony Lodge again. We will be shown to the sitting room. There, we will recover the photograph."

We had reached the door of 221B and were just about to enter when someone from the crowded street called out, "Good night, Mr. Holmes."

Sherlock and I turned, but we could not see who had spoken to us. "I've heard that voice before," said Holmes, looking down the street. "Who on earth could it have been?"

The next morning, the King arrived. As we rode to Briony Lodge in his carriage, we told him what had happened.

"Irene Adler is married," explained Holmes.

"Married! When? To whom?" cried the King.

"To an English lawyer named Norton," replied Holmes.

"She could not love him," answered our royal companion.

"I hope she does," said Holmes. "If she loves her husband, that means she does not love you. If she doesn't love you, she probably won't bother you again."

We were soon at Briony Lodge. As we approached the house, an elderly woman opened the front door and greeted us. "Mr. Sherlock Holmes, I believe?" she said.

"Yes. I am Holmes." My companion looked puzzled. It was an expression I did not see on his face very often.

"Madame Norton told me you would be here," the woman said. "She left for Europe this morning with her husband, never to return to England."

"And the photograph? The letters?" asked the

King with a groan. "All is lost!"

"We shall see," said Holmes. We entered the house and rushed to the sitting room. Holmes went to the hidden panel and opened it. He reached in and pulled out a photograph and a letter. The photograph was of Irene Adler. The letter was addressed to Sherlock Holmes. My friend tore open the envelope and read the letter inside:

Dear Mr. Holmes,

I congratulate you on a job well done. You almost had me completely fooled. Someone had warned me that the King would ask for your help. But even with the warning, you still managed to fool me into showing you where the photograph was.

It was only after the alarm that I began to suspect things were not as they seemed.

I wanted to make sure it was you, so I followed you and your companion home. As a stage performer, I have my own disguises and costumes. So I dressed myself as a young boy. When you arrived at Baker Street, I knew for sure that I was dealing with the great detective, Sherlock Holmes. It was careless of me, but I could not resist wishing you a good night.

My husband and I decided to leave right away. As for the photograph, tell His Majesty he has nothing to fear. He treated me badly. But my husband and I love each other. I will not use the photograph against him. But I will keep it to protect me from anything the King might do. He may want something to remember me by, so I am leaving this photograph.

Very truly yours,
Mrs. Irene Norton

"Oh, if only she and I could have married," cried the King. "What a queen she would have made! Mr. Holmes, I am in your debt. I have nothing to fear from the photograph. Now, tell me how I can reward you."

"There is one thing Your Majesty has that I would like," said Holmes.

"Name it!" the King replied.

"This photograph," answered Holmes.

Sherlock took the photograph of Irene Adler and bowed to the King. Then we left Briony Lodge. All the way home, Holmes was strangely quiet. The King had been saved from a scandal. But my friend had been *fooled* by a very unusual woman: Irene Adler.

The Redheaded League

⌒

It was a cool, autumn day when I decided to visit my friend Sherlock Holmes. The walk was pleasant and I was soon at Baker Street. But Holmes already had company. His visitor was a large, older man with hair as red as fire.

"You are just in time, Watson," said Holmes. "I believe you will find this gentleman's tale most interesting. It could prove what I have told you all along—that truth is stranger than fiction. And that the smallest of crimes are sometimes the most interesting.

"This is Mr. Jabez Wilson, who was telling me about some most unusual events. Please, Mr. Wilson, be so kind as to begin again."

Before the red-haired man began to tell his tale, he pulled a newspaper from his coat pocket. As he scanned the newspaper, I looked at him carefully. I tried to guess things about him, the way my detective friend always did.

Holmes could see what I was doing. He looked at me and said, "Watson, I see nothing, either. Except of course that our Mr. Wilson is a laborer, that he is a member of the organization known as the Freemasons, that he has visited China, and that he has been writing a lot recently."

Mr. Wilson looked up from the newspaper with wide eyes. "How on earth did you know that, Mr. Holmes? It's true that I was a laborer. I used to be a ship's carpenter. And the rest is all true, too."

Holmes explained, "The muscles of your right

hand are larger than your left. That tells me you used your hands in your work. You are wearing a pin with the symbol of the Freemasons. I see that the cuff of your right sleeve is very shiny and worn, a sign that you have spent a lot of time writing.

"Also," he continued, "there is a tattoo of a fish on your right wrist. I have studied tattoos. That one could only have been done in China. I also see a Chinese coin hanging from your watch chain. These things tell me you have been to that distant land."

I was always amazed by the store of facts in Holmes' head. He might not know that the earth circled the sun, or be able to name the author of a famous book. But he could tell you what country a certain tattoo came from. Or he could study the ash of different cigarettes and tell them apart.

Mr. Wilson laughed loudly. "I understand now, Mr. Holmes. At first, I thought you had done something difficult. But now I see how easy it was."

"Watson, remind me not to explain my methods in the future," he said to me with a grin. "And now, Mr. Wilson, have you found the item in the newspaper?"

"Yes. Here it is. This is what started it all." Wilson handed me the two-month-old paper. He pointed to a small notice on the page, which I read:

To the Redheaded League:

At the request of the late Ezekiah Hopkins, of Lebanon, Pennsylvania, U.S.A., employment is available to a redheaded man who is of sound body and mind, and is above the age of 21. The successful applicant will receive a salary. Please apply in person on Monday, at eleven o'clock, to Duncan Ross, at 7 Pope's Court, Fleet Street.

"What on earth does this mean?" I asked.

"Well, Mr. Watson," Wilson said, "I have a

small pawnshop where I buy and sell used items from people. I barely make enough to live on. I wouldn't even be able to pay my helper, except that he is willing to work for half of what I should be paying him, just so he can learn the business.

"His name is Vincent Spaulding, and he's a fine worker. My only complaint is that he spends too much time with his hobby—photography. He takes pictures, then spends hours in his darkroom in the shop basement.

"There is also a young girl in the shop. She does some cooking and cleaning. I'm not married and have no family. So it is just the three of us, living quietly.

"But then, two months ago," he continued, "Spaulding showed me the notice you just read. He said he wished he had red hair because he had heard the job was easy and paid well. He also heard that Ezekiah Hopkins was an American millionaire. It seemed that Hopkins had red hair and was an odd fellow. He had wanted his fortune to go to men with red hair. So, when he died, he left money to be given to them in this odd way.

"Spaulding explained that Hopkins had lived in London years ago. It seems he loved the place. So the money was left only for red-haired men from this city. My assistant said that the offer seemed perfect for me.

"So," continued Mr. Wilson, "we closed the shop and made our way to the offices of the League. Well, Mr. Holmes, when we arrived the streets were filled with redheaded men. I never knew there were so many of us. And all these men were in search of the job.

"I didn't think I had a chance. But Spaulding told me the position was only for a man with hair as fiery red as mine. So we pushed through the crowd to the office door and waited. It wasn't long before we were inside.

"In the office was a man with hair as red as

mine, sitting at a table. He spoke with each man, one after the other. He asked them all questions and then told them they were not suitable for the post.

"Finally, it was my turn. Right away, the man seemed very interested in me. He even asked everyone else to leave. He complimented my hair. To make sure I was right for the position, he even grabbed it with both hands and pulled at it! When I yelled in pain, he explained that he had to be careful. He said that many men had worn red wigs or had dyed their hair.

"Then he shook my hand and told me I had the job. He walked over to the office window, opened it, and yelled to the crowd that the position was filled.

"His name was Duncan Ross," said Wilson. "He told me I would need to work from ten in the morning until two in the afternoon. I explained that I had a shop to run. But Spaulding told us he would be happy to look after the business for me.

"I was told that my task would be to copy the Encyclopedia Britannica. I was to start the very next day.

"And so there I was the next day," said Wilson. "And as odd as it sounds, everything was as promised. Mr. Ross was there to get me started. I began copying the encyclopedia, starting with the letter A. Mr. Ross left me alone at times. And then, at two o'clock, he returned and told me I was finished for the day. He paid me and I went home.

"And so, Mr. Holmes, this continued week after week. I did my copying between ten and two. Every Saturday, I was paid. After a while, I did not see Mr. Ross very much. This continued for eight weeks. I wrote about archery and armor and architecture. And I was hoping to get to the letter B. But today, everything came to an end."

Mr. Wilson looked upset as he went on with

his story. "This morning, I went to the office as usual. But the door was locked. A small sign hung on the door. You can read it yourself." He handed Holmes the sign. It read:

The Redheaded League is no more. October 9, 1890.

"Mr. Wilson," said Holmes, "your case is most unusual. Please continue. What did you do next?"

"I asked the landlord if he knew where Mr. Ross had gone," answered Wilson. "The landlord said he didn't know a Mr. Ross. But he said the red-haired gentleman who had rented the office had moved to a new office, at 17 King Edward Street.

"Well, I went to that address, Mr. Holmes. But it was a factory and not an office. So I went home. Spaulding suggested that I would probably hear from the League. But I decided to come here. I thought perhaps you could help."

"You were right in coming to me, Mr. Wilson," said Holmes. "This is a remarkable case.

It may be far more serious than you imagine. Tell me, how long had your assistant Spaulding been working for you when he showed you the advertisement?"

"About a month," replied Wilson.

"And how did you come to hire him?"

"I put an advertisement in the paper," Wilson said. "Many people applied, but I gave Spaulding the job because he was willing to work for half of what I was paying."

"Can you describe him to me?" asked Holmes.

"He's small, but with a solid build. He is clean-shaven and has a white mark on his forehead, from an accident with acid."

Holmes sat up in his chair. "And his ears, are they pierced for earrings?"

"As a matter of fact, they are, Mr. Holmes."

"I have heard enough, Mr. Wilson," my friend said. "Today is Saturday. I hope to have an answer for you by Monday."

After Jabez Wilson had left, Holmes sat down in his chair and said to me, "Watson, I must ask you not to speak to me for fifty minutes." With that, he closed his eyes and sat without moving. I thought my companion had fallen asleep. Then, suddenly, he jumped up from his chair.

"Can your patients spare you for a few hours, Watson?" he asked.

"Yes, of course," I answered.

"Good. Then come with me," he said, and we headed out the door.

Before long, Sherlock Holmes and I were standing in front of Wilson's shop. My friend walked up the quiet street, then down, looking carefully at all the houses. He stopped in front of the shop again. With his walking stick, he tapped loudly on the sidewalk. Finally, he went to the shop door and knocked. A young, clean-shaven man answered.

"I'm sorry to bother you," said Holmes, "but

could you tell me how to get to the Strand from here?"

The man gave Holmes directions, then closed the door. My friend turned to me and said, "Watson, I know this gentleman. There are few who are smarter or more daring. Did you notice the knees of his pants?"

"No. What did you see?" I asked.

"Exactly what I expected to see," Holmes replied.

I pointed to the ground and asked, "But why did you tap on the sidewalk?"

"Before I answer any more questions, we must explore some more." I followed Holmes around the corner to the street behind Mr. Wilson's shop. It was a busy avenue, filled with traffic.

"Do you see the buildings here, Watson? I try to remember as much about the streets of London as possible," said Holmes. "There is Mortimer's tobacco shop, a newspaper shop, then the City and Suburban Bank, a restaurant, and McFarlane's carriage shop. Most interesting."

He then turned to me and said, "There is nothing more to do here, my friend. Shall we spend the afternoon enjoying a concert at St. James Hall? It is nearby and will be a welcome change." His suggestion didn't surprise me, as I knew Holmes enjoyed music very much. In fact, he was very skilled with the violin and often played for me.

As I watched him enjoying the concert, I thought about his various moods. When he was hard at work on a case, he was serious, determined, and cold. As he listened to the music that afternoon, he was lighthearted, happy, and dreamy, as if he hadn't a care in the world. But I also knew that his happy moods often meant he had solved a case. If I were a criminal, I'm not sure which of Holmes' moods I would prefer.

Outside the hall, a refreshed Holmes turned

to me. "Watson, I believe we are just in time to stop a serious crime. I will need your help tonight. Would you please bring your gun and meet me at Baker Street at ten o'clock? Thank you. And now, I have work to do."

As I watched Holmes hurry off, I began to think about the case of the Redheaded League. I had heard everything that my companion had heard. I had seen everything he had seen. But Sherlock Holmes saw that a serious crime was taking place, and I did not. Where could we be going tonight? What could we be doing? What crime was being committed? I would have to wait before finding out the answers to these questions.

When I arrived at Baker Street that night, I found two horse-drawn carriages outside. Inside, Holmes had already been joined by a police officer and another man.

"Ah, Watson. I believe you know Mr. Peter Jones of Scotland Yard. And this," he said, pointing to the other gentleman, "is Mr. Merry-weather, director of the City and Suburban Bank. He will be joining us on our adventure tonight."

"I hope our adventure won't be a wild goose chase," said Mr. Merryweather.

"Don't worry," replied Jones. "I have worked with Mr. Holmes before. He has helped Scotland Yard once or twice in the past. He might very well make a good detective someday."

Holmes said with a smile, "I promise you both that tonight will be worth the trouble. It will mean a large sum of money to you, Mr. Merryweather. And to you, Mr. Jones, it will mean the arrest of someone you've been after for many years."

"It's true, Mr. Merryweather," said Mr. Jones. "From what Mr. Holmes has told me, the shop assistant who calls himself Spaulding is none other than John Clay, whom I've been after for a long time now. He is a murderer and a thief.

There is no criminal in London I would rather put in jail."

The four of us left the apartment. Mr. Jones and Mr. Merryweather took one carriage. Holmes and I took the other. We were soon at the bank we had seen that afternoon. Mr. Merryweather led us into the building. We followed him through a series of doors, corridors, and down a number of stairs. Finally, we entered a large room, full of crates and boxes.

"This room seems remarkably safe from thieves," remarked Holmes.

"Very safe," said Mr. Merryweather, tapping the stone floor with his walking stick. "What's this? The floor sounds hollow!"

"Quiet, please!" instructed Holmes angrily. "Or you will give us away." My friend pulled out his magnifying glass and got down on his knees. He examined the floor carefully. Then he stood up and turned to me.

"Watson," he said, "by now you have guessed that we are in the basement of the City and Suburban Bank. What you don't know is that this bank recently received a large shipment of gold from the Bank of France. In fact, the crates in this room are filled with gold. Unfortunately, we are not the only ones who know this. That is why we are here tonight.

"And now," said Holmes, "we wait. Please hide behind these crates. We must be prepared for anything. Watson, have you your gun? Excellent. if you hear a shot, do not hesitate to fire back."

Holmes closed the cover of the lantern, and the room went completely black. We waited in silence. My arms and legs began to ache as I crouched behind a crate. We waited for over an hour, but it felt much longer to me.

Suddenly a faint spark of light came from the floor. The spark grew larger until we could see it was light shining through a hole in the floor. The hole opened and a hand came into sight. The hand pushed a large stone to one side. Then the face of a man appeared. The man pulled himself up and turned to help another man. The second man had a full head of very red hair.

At that moment, Sherlock Holmes jumped out and grabbed the first man. The redheaded man jumped back in the hole, just beyond the reach of Jones. The first man pulled out a gun, but Holmes knocked it out of his hand and it fell to the floor with a clatter.

"It's no use, John Clay," said Holmes calmly. "We have you."

"So I see," John Clay replied with a grim smile. "But you've let my partner escape."

"On the contrary," said Holmes. "There are three policemen at the other end of your tunnel. I'm certain they have him by

now. Mr. Jones, would you be so kind as to put Mr. Clay in handcuffs?"

"You will address me as 'sir,' if you don't mind," said Clay. "And you will say 'please.' I have royal blood in my veins, after all."

"Well, then," said Jones, "would you please, sir, follow me upstairs. A carriage is waiting to take Your Highness to the police station."

"That's better," said Clay smugly. He bowed to the three of us as Peter Jones led him away.

Back at Baker Street, Holmes filled me in on the details of the case. "You see, Watson, the reason for the Redheaded League was clear to me from the start. The League and the copying of the encyclopedia were all an excuse to get Mr. Wilson out of his shop for a few hours every day.

"First, Mr. Clay made sure he got a job with Mr. Wilson by offering to work for half pay. Then he and his red-haired partner put the ad in the paper. Mr. Clay made sure that Mr. Wilson saw the ad and applied for the position."

"But how could you guess what they were up to?" I asked.

"I knew there was nothing of value in the shop itself. Then I recalled that Mr. Wilson said his assistant spent a lot of time in the basement. In fact, he would stay down there for many hours a day. It was clear to me that he was digging a tunnel to another building. When Mr. Clay came to the door, the worn and dirty knees of his pants told me I was correct."

Holmes continued, "Mr. Wilson's shop was on a street with nothing but houses. I knew Clay wasn't tunneling to any of them. When I tapped on the sidewalk in front of the shop, I was testing for a tunnel. When I did not detect one, I knew that the tunnel was at the back.

"Now, to where was he digging?" Holmes said.

"When I saw the street behind the shop, I saw the City and Suburban Bank right away. It was right across from the back of Mr. Wilson's shop. I knew the bank was the target of Mr. Clay's efforts."

"But how did you know they would move tonight?" I asked.

"Clay and his partner closed the office of the Redheaded League," Holmes explained. "This told me they no longer needed Mr. Wilson out of the shop. It meant they had finished the tunnel. Next, I guessed that they would spring into action as soon as possible. I was sure they would move tonight, Saturday night. That way, the robbery would not be noticed until the bank opened on Tuesday morning. By then Mr. Clay, his partner, and the gold would be long gone."

"Well done," I said with admiration. "It was a long chain of events from the newspaper ad to tonight's arrest. And each link was figured out perfectly. The people of London should be grateful to you, Holmes."

"I don't do it for the thanks, my dear Watson," said Holmes with a slight smile. "It is the challenge that is important to me."

The Adventure of the Blue Carbuncle

∽

Two days after Christmas, I decided to visit Sherlock Holmes. I wanted to wish him a merry Christmas. When I arrived at Baker Street, I found my friend resting on the sofa. Next to him, an old, worn, dirty hat was slouched over the back of a chair. I saw a magnifying glass sitting on a nearby table.

"I suppose this hat has something to do with a crime?" I asked.

"No, my dear Watson," answered Holmes. "Not a crime. Just one of those odd little events that take place in a large city like London. I received the hat on Christmas morning from a policeman named Peterson. He told me he was walking home on Christmas Eve when he saw a man wearing this hat and carrying a goose over his shoulder."

"No doubt for his Christmas dinner," I said.

"No doubt, Watson," Holmes replied. "Peterson then explained that a group of thugs appeared and began to bother the man. They pushed him and knocked off his hat. The man tried to defend himself by swinging his cane and accidentally broke a store window.

"That's when Peterson ran to help the poor stranger. When the gang saw Peterson coming, they ran. But their victim ran, too. The old man must have thought Peterson would arrest him for breaking the window.

"And so the officer was left with the hat and the goose. A piece of paper was tied to the bird. It read: 'For Mrs. Henry Baker.' And the initials 'H. B.' are on the hat. But there must be hundreds of Henry Bakers in London. It would be impossible to find the right Henry Baker and return his hat and goose to him.

"Peterson knows that I am interested in even the smallest problem," said Holmes. "So he brought the items to me. Since I couldn't keep the goose forever, Peterson came back and took it for his dinner tonight. Meanwhile, I have been learning about the stranger by studying his hat."

"But what can you possibly learn from examining a hat?" I exclaimed.

"You know how I work, Watson," Holmes replied. "Here is my magnifying glass. You tell me what you can discover about our stranger."

I took the hat and looked it over. It was an ordinary black hat, but it had become worn with age. The red silk lining was faded. I saw the initials "H. B." inside. There were holes in the brim for an

elastic band to hold the hat on the wearer's head. But the elastic was missing. The hat was cracked, dusty, and had worn spots all over it. Someone had colored the spots with ink.

"I can see nothing," I said, handing the hat back to my friend.

"On the contrary, Watson. You see everything. But you don't understand the meaning of what you see."

"Then what can you tell me about the hat's owner?" I asked.

Holmes explained, "Three years ago the owner was a fairly wealthy man. But since then, he has become much poorer. He was a careful person, but isn't anymore. Something has caused these changes. Perhaps he is gambling. This may be why his wife no longer loves him.

"Despite all this, our stranger is still careful about his appearance. But he doesn't go out much. He is middle-aged and not in the best of health. He has gray hair, cut within the last few days, to which he applies a cream. And he probably uses candles to light his home."

"You must be joking, Holmes," I said.

"Not at all, my good Watson. This hat was very fashionable three years ago. It is also expensive. So our stranger must have had enough money to buy it then. I know he is not as wealthy as before because he can't afford to buy a new one now, even though it is old and worn.

"I know he was a careful person once, because he went to the trouble of having the hat fitted with the elastic. But the elastic probably broke. He never replaced it because he is not as careful as he used to be.

"I know he still cares about his appearance," Holmes continued, "because he tries to hide the worn spots on his hat with ink. Look closely at the lining and you will see tiny hair clippings. These tell me the owner's age and hair color. They also tell me he got his hair cut recently. And you can smell the hair cream."

Holmes went on. "The dust on the hat isn't the type you would find outside. It is the sort that collects inside a house. That tells me he spends more time at home than anywhere else. The perspiration marks inside tell me the man perspires even when walking, which means he is not very fit."

"But," I interrupted, "you also said his wife stopped loving him."

"This hat has not been brushed for weeks," replied Holmes. "What loving wife would let her husband leave the house with such a dusty hat upon his head?"

"But he might be a bachelor," I said.

"You forget the note attached to the goose. It said: 'To Mrs. Henry Baker.'"

"I see. But how on earth do you know that he uses candles to light his house and not gas?"

"There are many wax stains on his hat," Holmes replied. "We would not see those if his house were lit with gas."

Just then, our door flew open and the policeman Peterson rushed in. "Mr. Holmes!" he cried out. "Look what my wife found inside the goose she was preparing for dinner!" Peterson held out his hand toward us. In it, he held a beautiful, blue gemstone. It was slightly smaller than a bean, but it shone and twinkled like a brilliant blue star.

"Mr. Peterson!" exclaimed Holmes. "I would recognize that stone anywhere. It is the Countess of Morcar's precious blue carbuncle!"

"Do you mean the jewel that was stolen?" I asked.

"Correct, Watson," was Holmes' answer. "It went missing just five days ago, at the Hotel Cosmopolitan. I have been reading about it in the newspaper. The police arrested a plumber named John Horner. He is being charged with its theft.

"It seems that James Ryder, the hotel manager, let Horner into the Countess' room to fix the plumbing. When Mr. Ryder returned, the plumber was gone and the gem was missing. Catherine Cusack, the Countess' maid, told the police the same story. The police were alerted right away and Horner was arrested that evening. They didn't find the missing gem. And the plumber insists he is innocent.

"So," continued Holmes, "how did the stone get from the Countess to us? We know that it came from the goose, which belonged to Henry Baker. I would say that our first step is to find Mr. Baker. And we can do that by putting a notice in the newspaper."

Holmes took pencil and paper, and spoke as he wrote. "Found at the corner of Goodge Street, a goose and black hat belonging to Mr. Henry Baker. Please claim both at 6:30 this evening at 221B Baker Street."

"And now, Mr. Peterson," Holmes said, "would you be so kind as to do two things for me? Take this message and place it in all the evening newspapers. And second, please bring us back another goose for Mr. Baker!"

When Peterson had gone, Holmes held the carbuncle to the light. "Watson, this stone was only discovered twenty years ago. It was found on the banks of the Amoy River in southern China. It is very valuable because most stones like it are ruby red and not blue. And like all valuable gems, this one leaves a trail of crime wherever it goes. There have been two murders and many robberies committed because of it already. I will put it away safely and let the Countess know we have her precious pebble."

"And what do you make of the plumber, John Horner? And Henry Baker?" I asked.

"I don't know anything about Horner, my

good fellow. And I don't think Mr. Baker is guilty of anything. But we will test that when he answers our notice. Please join me this evening, Watson. With any luck, we will be able to question him about his bird."

That evening, Henry Baker arrived at our place in search of his lost goose. He was a large man, with a broad face and brown beard. He gave me the impression that he was an educated man. But his worn clothes showed that he had fallen on hard times.

"I am curious," Holmes began. "Why didn't you put a notice about your lost items in the newspaper?"

"Well, Mr. Holmes," Baker replied, "I don't have as much money as I used to. And I was sure the thieves had taken the goose. So I thought it would be a waste of money to pay for a notice."

"I understand," said my friend. "By the way,

Mr. Baker, I am afraid that we have eaten your goose. It would have gone bad had we waited too long . . ."

Our visitor let out a groan and looked very disappointed.

"But don't worry. We bought you another one." Holmes pointed to the bird, which was sitting on a table. "Of course, we still have the feathers and bones of your goose, if you want them."

"Now, why would I want that?" laughed Mr. Baker. "No, I'll just take this goose and be on my way."

"Very well," said Holmes, as he looked at me with raised eyebrows. "Oh, by the way, Mr. Baker, I wonder if you could tell me where you got your delicious bird. I should like to know where to get another."

"Well, Mr. Holmes," he said, "there is a group of us who are regulars at the Alpha Inn. The owner of the inn started a 'goose club.' Every week for the past year, we all paid a small amount of money. So, by the end of the year, there was enough to buy each man a goose for Christmas. That's where I got it. And now, if you don't mind, I'll take this bird and finally enjoy a proper Christmas dinner."

After our visitor had left, Holmes and I followed up this lead. We left and made our way through the cold London streets to the Alpha Inn. Inside, we found a quiet table and ordered two glasses of hot apple cider from the owner.

"I hope your cider is as good as your geese," Holmes said.

"My geese?" said the owner as he poured out the warm beverage.

"Yes. I was just speaking to Mr. Henry Baker about them."

"Oh, well, they're not my geese," said the owner. "I got them from a gentleman down in Covent Garden. Breckinridge is his name."

Holmes and I finished our cider and made our way to Covent Garden Market. Just as he was closing his stall for the night, we found Mr. Breckinridge.

"Sold out, I see," said Holmes to Breckinridge. "That's too bad. By any chance, can you tell me where you get your birds from?"

To our surprise, Holmes' question made the bird seller angry. "Now look, mister," he said loudly. "What are you getting at? You're not the first person today to bother me about my geese. 'Where are they?' and 'Who did you sell them to?' I never heard such a fuss being made over some fowl."

"I'm sorry," said Holmes. "It's just that I had made a bet that the geese in question were raised in the country."

"Well, you've lost your bet then, mister," said Breckinridge. "They were raised in town. Here, look at my record book—it shows who I bought

the geese from. And it shows who I sold them to.
And the birds I sold to the Alpha Inn were raised
by a Mrs. Oakshott. And it says right here she lives
on Brixton Road, in London!"

Holmes and I left Mr. Breckinridge to finish
closing his stall. We stood in the street, wondering whether to visit Mrs. Oakshott right away or
wait until morning. Just then, we heard shouting.
It was coming from Mr. Breckinridge. He was
yelling at a small man. "Stop bothering me. I've
had enough questions about my geese today! Go
and ask Mrs. Oakshott about her geese!" Then he
turned and stomped away.

Holmes walked up to the small man and said,
"Excuse me. My name is Sherlock Holmes and I
believe my friend and I can help you. I take it you
are looking for some geese. They were sold by
Mrs. Oakshott to Mr. Breckinridge. He, in turn,
sold them to the Alpha Inn. From the inn, one of
the geese went to Mr. Henry Baker."

"Mr. Holmes, you can't imagine how important it is to me that I find my goose," exclaimed the man.

"In that case," said Holmes, "please come to my quarters where we can talk. Mister . . . ?"

"My name is John Robinson," answered the stranger.

"No, no, I mean your real name," said Holmes with a smile. "I insist."

The stranger's face turned red, and he looked very uncomfortable. "Well," he said, "my real name is James Ryder."

"That's better," said Holmes. "Much better, Mr. Ryder, of the Hotel Cosmopolitan."

Back in our rooms, Holmes, Ryder, and I warmed ourselves by the fire. "And now, Mr. Ryder," Holmes began, "you wish to know the whereabouts of Mrs. Oakshott's geese. Or should I say, one special goose. The white one with the black mark on its tail."

"Yes," cried James Ryder, "can you tell me where it went?"

"It came here. And it was a remarkable bird indeed. In fact, after it was dead, it laid an egg. The brightest little blue egg you have ever seen." Holmes held out his hand and showed our guest the blue carbuncle. Ryder stared at it. He sprang from his chair and the color drained from his face.

"The game's up, Ryder," proclaimed Holmes. "I know most of what happened. The police might treat you better if you now tell us what you know."

Ryder looked as if he would faint, so I helped him back into his chair. "It was Catherine Cusack," he answered, "the Countess' maid. She told me about the gem."

"And you decided to steal it," said Holmes. "You knew that the plumber, John Horner, had been in trouble with the police before. So you arranged for him to be in the Countess' room. When he left, you stole the stone. Then you called the police, told them about Horner, and they arrested him."

"Please, Mr. Holmes," pleaded Ryder. "Have mercy! I was never in trouble before. I'll never do it again! Please!"

"Really, Mr. Ryder," said Holmes. "You ask for forgiveness. But you were ready to send Mr. Horner to prison for a crime you committed. Enough! Tell us the rest of the story."

Ryder returned to his tale. "When Horner was arrested, I was worried that the police might question me. I was afraid they would search me for the item. So I went to my sister's house . . ."

"Mrs. Oakshott," said Holmes.

"Yes," said Ryder. "I went there and thought about what to do next. I remembered an old friend who had spent time in prison. I knew he could help me sell the jewel. So I decided I would go to Kilburn, where he lives. But I was still worried the police might find the stone on me.

"I was sitting in my sister's backyard. It was full of the geese she raises. That's when it came to me. My sister had promised me one of her birds as a Christmas present. I decided I would stuff the carbuncle down its throat. Then I would take it with me. If the police stopped me, they would never think to look inside the goose.

"So I caught one of the birds, the one with the black mark on its tail. I held open its bill and stuffed the stone down its throat. My sister came out and asked me what I was doing. Just then, I lost hold of the bird and it flapped its way back to the others. I told her I was going to take my Christmas present. So she caught and killed it, and I went to Kilburn.

"Imagine my horror," Ryder continued, "when I opened up the bird for my friend and found nothing. There had been some terrible mistake. I rushed back to town and ran to my sister's. I burst into her backyard, only to find all the birds gone. She had sent them to the dealer, Breckinridge. I asked her if there had been another goose with a black mark on its tail. She told me yes. I had taken the wrong bird!

"I ran to Covent Garden as quickly as I could. But Breckinridge would not tell me where my bird had gone. So here I am. I have committed a terrible crime." Ryder burst into tears and buried his face in his hands.

There was a long silence. Sherlock Holmes tapped his fingers on the table. Then he stood up and threw open the door that looked out onto the street.

"Get out!" he said.

In an instant, Ryder ran out the door and disappeared into the night.

"Perhaps I'm making a mistake," said Holmes.

"But I don't believe Mr. Ryder will stray from the law again. Besides, Horner will be set free. The blue carbuncle will be returned. In the end, we have saved him from a life in prison.

"After all," Holmes said, "we have had a most interesting problem to solve—for which I am rather grateful to the foolish man. . . . Aren't you, my dear Watson?"

The Adventure of the Speckled Band

⁓

I'm sorry to wake you, Watson," whispered Holmes as he stood over me, "but we have a visitor. There is a young woman in the sitting room who wants to see us. I'm sure it's important if she's come at this hour. Would you care to join me?"

"My dear Holmes," I replied sleepily, "I wouldn't miss it for the world."

With my wife out of town, I was staying with Holmes for the evening. I always enjoyed helping my colleague in his investigations. It was fascinating to watch him gather clues and use them to solve crimes. So I dressed quickly and joined him in the sitting room. We beheld a woman dressed in black, wearing a veil over her face.

"Good morning, madam," began my companion. "My name is Sherlock Holmes. This is my friend and partner, Dr. Watson. How can we be of service to you?"

The woman lifted the veil from her face. We could see that she was pale and upset. "I am very frightened, Mr. Holmes," she began.

"We will try our best to help you," Holmes said, trying to calm her. "I see that you traveled to London by train this morning. And that you rode to the train station in a horse-drawn wagon."

"How do you know that?" she asked with a look of surprise on her face.

"The return ticket is tucked into your glove," Holmes explained. "And the left arm of your jacket is splashed with fresh mud. You could only have gotten splashed that way by sitting on the left-hand side of an open wagon."

"You're correct," she replied. "I have traveled all this way because I am going mad, Mr. Holmes. I have no one to turn to. You must help me."

"Please, madam. Tell us your problem." Holmes sat back in his chair, closed his eyes, and listened.

"My name is Helen Stoner. I live with my step-father, Dr. Grimesby Roylott. He is the last member of an old family. They were wealthy once. But over the years, the Roylotts lost their fortune. All that remains is the family home, Stoke Moran.

"Years ago, my step-father lived in India and had a successful medical practice. That is where he met and married my mother.

My twin sister Julia and I were only two at the time.

"It was in India that my stepfather's troubles began," she said. "In a fit of anger, he got into a fight, killed someone, and spent many years in prison. When my stepfather was released, we moved back to England, where he returned to being a doctor. But he was a changed man by then.

"Shortly after our return, my mother passed away, leaving all her money to my stepfather. My sister and I would receive some money of our own, but only when we got married. With my mother gone, we left London and went to live in Stoke Moran."

Miss Stoner grew more upset as she continued her story. "My stepfather became even more troubled after that. His temper grew, and later he was arrested by the police for fighting. People became afraid of him. His only friends were a group of poor travelers who roamed the countryside and sometimes visited Stoke Moran. He would often let them camp in the woods near the house.

"His behavior grew stranger with every passing day," she continued. "He loves wild animals. So he brought a wild cheetah and a baboon from India, letting them run wild in the woods around our home.

"My sister Julia and I became very unhappy. No servants would stay with us. So my sister and I took care of that big house by ourselves. It was very hard for us. Julia was thirty when she died, but she looked much older."

"Your sister is dead?" asked Holmes.

"Yes," our visitor replied. "She died two years ago. And it is her death that I wish to speak to you about. Just before that sad event, Julia became engaged. My stepfather did not object. But just before the wedding, a terrible thing happened."

When Holmes heard this, he opened his eyes and looked at our visitor. "Do not leave out any details," he said.

Miss Stoner continued. "My stepfather, sister, and I lived in only one part of the old house. Julia's bedroom was between mine and my stepfather's, on the main floor. There are no doors connecting the rooms. But they all share the same hallway. The windows of the rooms look out on the yard.

"That night two years ago, all three of us were in our rooms. While I was still awake, my sister came to me. She said she could smell my stepfather's cigar smoke and that it bothered her. So we sat and talked about her wedding until about eleven o'clock. That's when she got up to return to her room.

"As she was leaving, Julia asked me if I had heard a whistling sound at night. She told me she had heard such a sound for the last few nights, but she did not know where the noise had come from.

"I told her it might have been the travelers who were camped nearby. I sleep more soundly than she, which may explain why I heard nothing. After that, we said good night. My sister returned to her room and I heard her lock her door."

"Did you always lock your doors?" asked Holmes.

"Yes," answered Miss Stoner. "We were afraid of my father's wild animals."

"Continue," said Holmes.

"Well, that night," she went on, "I could not sleep, and lay awake for hours. Suddenly, I heard Julia scream. I jumped from my bed and ran into the hallway. At that moment, I heard a quiet whistle, followed by a loud clanging sound.

"In the hallway, I watched as Julia's bedroom

door opened. My dear sister slowly stepped from her room. I saw terror in her eyes. She could barely stand, and she moved about as if she was in pain. I ran to her just as she fell to the floor. As I held her in my arms, she cried out, 'Oh, Helen! It was the band! The speckled band!' She reached out with one hand and pointed to my stepfather's room. I called out to him and he quickly appeared. But there was nothing we could do. That night, Julia died."

"And you are sure," asked Holmes, "that you heard the whistle and clanging sound of metal?"

"I think I did," Miss Stoner replied.

"I am sure a doctor examined your sister's body. What did he find?" asked Holmes.

"He knew of our stepfather's temper, Mr. Holmes, and was very careful, but he did not find what killed Julia. It is still a mystery. We know that Julia had locked both the windows and the bed-room door. We searched the room carefully, but couldn't find any hidden entrances. My sister must have been alone when she met her end. Besides, she didn't have any marks on her."

"What about poison?" asked Holmes.

"The doctor found no trace of it," replied the young woman. "Mr. Holmes, I believe she died of fright. And I think that when my sister said the word 'band,' she meant a 'band' of people. Like the band of travelers.

"Well, that was two years ago. I have come to see you, Mr. Holmes, because a month ago I became engaged also. Again, my stepfather did not object. My fiancé and I are to be married in the spring.

"But two days ago," she said with a fearful look on her face, "work began on some walls of our house. And because of the repairs, I had to move into my sister's bedroom. As you can imagine, I did not feel comfortable. Then, last night, as I lay in bed, I suddenly heard a noise. It was the sound of a quiet whistle! I jumped out of bed and lighted a lamp. I didn't see anything, but I was so scared that I dressed and dared not go back to bed. In the morning, I left the house and came to London to beg for your help."

"It was the right thing to do," said my friend. "But, Miss Stoner, you haven't told me everything about your stepfather."

"What do you mean?" she asked.

Holmes took the young woman's hand in his and held up her wrist. There were marks on her skin as if she had been grabbed by a very strong hand. Our visitor lowered her head and said, "He is a troubled man, Mr. Holmes."

My friend became silent. He stared into the fire that warmed our room. "We don't have a moment to lose," he said finally. "Miss Stoner, if we come to your house today, can we see the rooms without your stepfather knowing?"

"Yes. He is visiting London today and won't be home," she replied.

"Good. Then Watson and I will take the train and meet you there this afternoon."

"Thank you, Mr. Holmes," she said. "I feel better already. Now, if that is all, I will see you this afternoon." Our visitor lowered the veil over her face and left.

"This is a strange and dangerous case, Holmes," I said. "From everything we have heard, Miss Stoner's sister must have been alone when she was killed. But what was the whistling sound? And what did the dead woman's last words mean?"

"It seems to me," my companion began, "that it must have something to do with the band of travelers. Also, it is clear that Dr. Roylott would have lost money if his daughters married. Clearly, he would prefer his daughters not to be wed. And the metal clang? Perhaps it was the shutter of the window opening."

"But if that is the case," I said, "how then did the travelers kill Miss Stoner? It doesn't quite make sense to me."

"I agree, Watson. And that is why we must visit Stoke Moran today."

Just then, the door flew open and a huge man burst into our room. He looked at Holmes and me with a wild, angry expression on his face.

"Which of you is Holmes?" he roared.

"I am," Holmes answered calmly. "And who are you?"

"I am Dr. Grimesby Roylott," he cried. "I know my stepdaughter has been here. And I know you as Mr. Sherlock Holmes, the trouble-maker. What did she say to you?"

Holmes laughed, "Please close the door on your way out, Dr. Roylott. It is cold outside."

"I'll go when I'm finished with you. I am a powerful man, Mr. Holmes. You had better stay out of my business. Or else!" Roylott grabbed the metal poker from the fireplace. He held the piece of metal in his hands and bent it as if it were rub-ber. He threw the twisted metal into the fireplace, took one last look at us, and stormed out.

"Well, Watson," Holmes began, "our investiga-tion has become much more interesting. I only hope the doctor's visit doesn't mean Miss Stoner is in even more danger. I think we must take ourselves to Stoke Moran right away. Let us go to the train station. And Watson, I think it would be a good idea if you brought your gun. I wouldn't want Dr. Roylott to treat us the way he treated that metal poker."

Holmes and I took the train from London to the town of Leatherhead. From there, we took a horse-drawn carriage. But before we reached Stoke Moran, we saw Miss Stoner walking through a field toward the road. She had come from her troubled home to meet us.

"I'm very happy you're here," she said to us after the carriage had gone. "Dr. Roylott is still in town and won't be back for a while."

"We have had the mixed pleasure of meeting your stepfather," explained Holmes. "He paid us a visit after you left."

"You mean he followed me?" she cried in fear.

"Yes," answered Holmes. "So we must be

very careful. And we must take a closer look at the rooms while we have a chance."

Stoke Moran was an old, gray, stone mansion. One side of the house looked empty. The windows on that side were broken and covered with boards. The other side looked well kept. Smoke from the chimneys told us that the family lived in this part of the house.

"I see that these are the bedroom windows," Holmes said, pointing to a set of three windows. "The doctor's, then your sister's, and then yours?"

"Yes," answered Miss Stoner. "And you can see where the workmen have been busy. But Mr. Holmes, I don't think the work was necessary. I think it was a way to get me to sleep in my sister's bedroom."

"Most interesting," said my companion. "Miss Stoner, please go into your sister's room while Watson and I stay out here. Make sure the window is locked."

The young woman went inside. Holmes pulled a knife from his pocket and tried to open the window from the outside. When he failed, he used his magnifying glass and looked at the window frame and the hinges. "No," he said finally, "no one could get in through these windows. Watson, let us continue our search for clues inside."

We joined Miss Stoner in her sister's room. Holmes sat down in a chair and silently studied everything around him. A rope hung from the ceiling down to the bed. It was a rope you would pull to ring a bell. The bell was a signal for servants. The rope was so long that the end rested on the pillow.

"Where is the bell that is rung by this bell-rope?" he asked.

"In the housekeeper's room," replied Miss Stoner.

"It looks new," observed Holmes. "Did your sister ask for it?"

"It is only a couple of years old. But no, my sister did not ask for it."

"Why would you need such a nice bell-rope here, I wonder?" said Holmes. He got up from the chair, pulled out his magnifying glass again, and got down on his hands and knees. He crawled back and forth over the floor, searching for clues. He then examined the walls in the same way.

Holmes walked over to the bed and studied the bell-rope. Finally, he grabbed it and pulled. "Why, it doesn't work," he said. "It is attached to a hook on the ceiling and doesn't ring a bell at all. This is most interesting. Also, the air vent on the ceiling is unusual." Holmes pointed to a small opening next to where the bell-rope reached the ceiling. "Has the air vent always been there, Miss Stoner?"

"No," she answered. "It was put in around the same time that the bell-rope was put in."

Next, we visited Dr. Roylott's bedroom. Holmes carefully examined the bed, a bookshelf, an armchair beside the bed, a wooden chair, a table, and a large metal safe. He noticed a small dish of milk sitting on the safe.

"Does Dr. Roylott keep a cat?" he asked.

"No," Miss Stoner replied.

My friend then bent down and studied the wooden chair. "Yes, that's it then," he said as he stood up. "But wait, what's this?" Holmes pointed at a rope, looped over one post of the bed. "Ah, Watson. It is a wicked world. Especially when a smart man turns to crime. I have seen enough, Miss Stoner. Let us leave these rooms."

Once outside, Holmes turned to the young woman. "It is very important that you do everything I tell you. Your life may depend on it. When Dr. Roylott returns, you must stay in your sister's room. Then, tonight, when you hear your stepfather in his bedroom, you must open your window. Put a lamp where it can be seen from outside. Then quietly leave and return to your own room. Be sure to lock the door.

"Watson and I will be watching. When we see the lamp, we will enter your sister's bedroom through the window. We will spend the night there."

"Mr. Holmes," said Miss Stoner, "I think you know what killed my sister. You must tell me! Did she die of fright?"

"No, I don't believe so," answered Holmes. "But until I know for sure, that is all I can tell you. I'm sorry. And now, Watson and I must leave before your stepfather returns. Do as I have instructed and all will be well."

My companion and I left Miss Stoner at Stoke Moran. There was an inn not far from the house where we were able to take a room. From there, we could look across a field and see the bedroom windows. We waited for night to fall.

"Watson," said Holmes as we sat looking out at the house, "I must warn you that we could be in danger tonight."

"Danger? But how?" I asked. "I didn't see anything this afternoon that suggested danger. You have clearly seen more than I have in these rooms."

"No, we have seen the same things," replied Holmes. "But I have reasoned out what those things mean. First, there is the air vent, which I expected to find. Miss Stoner said that her sister could smell her stepfather's cigar smoke the night she died. That told me there would be a vent connecting the two rooms. There is also the bell-rope that doesn't ring a bell. Plus the interesting fact that the air vent and the bell-rope were put in the room at the same time.

"What you may not have seen was an odd feature about the bed. It was clamped to the floor. That means you could not move the bed away from the bell-rope and air vent. Yes, Watson. We are dealing with a dreadful criminal. We may have a night of horrors ahead of us."

As the hours passed, the two of us watched the distant, dark house. Finally, a light appeared in a window. It was our signal. We left the inn and made our way through the fields. Suddenly, as we were crossing the lawn, a dark figure darted from the bushes. The creature's arms and legs flew wildly as it ran off into the shadows.

"My word!" I gasped. "What was *that*?"

Holmes laughed quietly. "This is a strange case indeed, Watson. That was the doctor's baboon. Now quickly. Let us climb in the bedroom window before we see the cheetah as well."

We crawled in through the open window and closed it behind us. Once inside, Holmes whispered to me. "Do not make a sound, Watson. I will sit on the bed. You sit in that chair. Have your gun ready." Holmes had brought a cane

with him, and he placed it on the bed. "We must sit in the dark. We do not want Dr. Roylott to see anything." He turned out the lamp, and we were in total darkness.

The hours passed as we waited silently. A church bell echoed in the distance. A bird called in the night. Then we heard a sound that could only come from a large, wild cat. It was the cheetah walking by the bedroom window.

After a long wait, my eyes caught a dim flicker of light from the air vent above the bed. The light quickly disappeared and was followed by the odor of burning oil. Someone had lighted a lamp in the next room. Next came the sound of movement, followed by silence.

A half hour passed before I heard something else. It was a quiet hissing sound, like steam from a boiling kettle. Suddenly, Holmes jumped from the bed. He struck a match, grabbed his cane, and swung it at the bell-rope. At the same time, I heard a low, whistling sound.

"Did you see it, Watson?" yelled Holmes. "Did you see it?"

My companion was looking up at the air vent. Just then, a loud cry filled Stoke Moran. It was a cry of pain and fear that turned into an angry shriek. As Holmes and I stared at each other, the cry faded away into silence.

We ran into the hallway, to the door of Dr. Roylott's room. Holmes knocked loudly. No one answered, so we opened the door and entered. The room was lit by the light of a lamp. We could see that the safe was open. Dr. Grimesby Roylott sat on the wooden chair that Holmes had studied earlier that day. The doctor was in his dressing gown and slippers. The coiled rope lay across his lap.

The doctor did not move. His head was turned toward the ceiling, and his eyes stared upward. Wrapped tightly around his head was a strange yellow band. It was covered with brown speckles.

"The band! The speckled band!" whispered Holmes.

As I took a step forward, the band began to move. Then the head and puffed-up collar of a snake rose up out of the doctor's hair.

"It is a swamp adder!" cried Holmes. "The deadliest snake in India. The doctor's murder weapon has turned on him. He has been bitten." Holmes took the rope and put it around the snake's collar. He tightened it and carefully conveyed the snake into the safe. "It is too late for us to do anything for him. But we must take Miss Stoner from this place, and call the police."

The next day, as Holmes and I returned to London by train, he explained the facts of the case to me. "At first, Watson, I was on the wrong track. I knew that Miss Stoner's sister had used the word 'band.' I also knew of the travelers who were camping nearby. So I thought the solution to the mystery lay with the band of travelers.

"But when we inspected the rooms, I realized that no one could have entered the locked bedroom. I also took note of the bell-rope, the air vent, and the bed that could not be moved. It became clear to me that the rope was a bridge between the bed and the air vent. Right away, I thought of a snake. If Dr. Roylott had a cheetah and a baboon, he might easily have a snake. As a doctor who practiced in India, he would also know that this snake's poison could not be detected. And he would know that its bite would be invisible.

"When his stepdaughter Julia became engaged," Holmes explained, "he did not want her to get the money. So he put the bell-rope in her room and had the air vent installed. Once they were in place, he waited until his stepdaughter was asleep. I could tell from looking at the chair in his room that he stood on it to reach the air vent. He would place the snake in the air vent. The deadly creature would crawl through the vent, down the rope, and onto the victim's bed.

"At first, the snake did not attack Julia Stoner. But the doctor had trained it to return at the sound of a whistle. That is what she heard. The milk also helped lure the snake back to Roylott's room. He would then catch it with the rope and put it in the safe. The clanging sound that the sisters heard was that of the safe being closed.

"And so, last night, I listened for the faintest sound that a snake could make. When I heard the hissing, I lit a match and attacked it. The creature quickly slithered back to Dr. Roylott's room. But I had hit it with my cane, making it angry. So when it returned to the doctor's bedroom, it attacked."

Sherlock Holmes looked out the window at

the English countryside. It was hard to imagine that last night's events had taken place in such a peaceful setting. "The murderer is dead," he said, "killed by his own strange murder weapon."

The Greek Interpreter

ᥱ

In all the years I had known him, Sherlock Holmes never spoke of his family. Perhaps this is why I sometimes saw him as a man without feelings. To Holmes, intelligence was more important than feelings of friendship and affection. With no friends or relatives, he was like a brain without a heart. So I was surprised when one day he began to talk about his brother.

It was a summer evening, and Holmes and I were resting after dinner. Our conversation wandered from topic to topic. Somehow, we started talking about the forces that shaped a person. We wondered if we inherited our character from our parents, the way a son might inherit his father's eyes, or a daughter her mother's hair. Or whether everything depended on how you were raised.

"Well, Holmes," I said, "it seems to me your parents raised you in such a way that you couldn't have been anything but the great detective you turned out to be."

"There is some truth in that, Watson," replied Holmes, "but I think it must run in the family. Take my older brother Mycroft. Though we were raised in the same way, his skills are much greater than mine, I assure you."

"Then why isn't he as well known as you?" I asked.

"He surely has stronger powers of observation and reasoning. But Mycroft isn't interested in the other things that are needed to do my work. He does not have the energy to gather clues or hunt down suspects. He can't be bothered to roam the countryside, testing his ideas. So instead, Mycroft uses his skill with numbers to take care of certain matters for the government.

"He is a creature of habit, Watson, and does the same things every day. In fact, if you would like to meet him, I would be happy to introduce him to you. He is always at the Diogenes Club at this time of day. We can walk over there now."

"I have never heard of the Diogenes Club," I said after we had left Baker Street.

"Few have," Holmes replied. "Its members are an odd group. They don't go to the club to meet other members. In fact, there is a rule that forbids them from talking to each other. No, they go there for the comfortable chairs and the newspapers. And because it is one of the few places where they can be alone."

We were soon at the Diogenes Club. Inside, I looked into a large room and saw a number of gentlemen sitting in armchairs. They were reading their newspapers. No one was speaking to anyone. Holmes explained that there was one room where conversation was allowed. He left me there, and I waited quietly. My friend soon returned with a large, heavyset man. It was his older brother, Mycroft Holmes. The brother's expression showed the same alertness as that of Holmes.

"I am glad to meet you, Dr. Watson," said Mycroft. "Thanks to your stories about my brother's adventures, he is quite famous. By the way, Sherlock, I expected to hear from you last week. I thought you might want to know my thoughts on the Manor House case. It was Adams, wasn't it?"

"Yes, it was Adams," said Holmes as we sat down.

"I hope you like our club, Dr. Watson," Mycroft said as he looked out the window at the traffic in the street. "It is an excellent place to observe people. For example, the two men walking toward us . . ."

Holmes glanced over and said, "The billiard player and the other gentleman?"

"Yes," replied Mycroft. "What do you make of the other?"

The two men stopped outside the window to talk. I could see chalk marks on the jacket of the first man. The chalk was clearly from playing a game of billiards. The other man was very small, with dark, tanned skin. He wore a hat and carried several packages under his arm.

"I would say he was a soldier," observed Holmes.

"He left the army recently," said Mycroft.

"Served in India . . ."

"An officer . . ."

"Royal Artillery, I would say," added Holmes.

"Ah, a widower," said Mycroft.

"But with a child, my dear Mycroft."

"Children, my dear Sherlock, children."

"Really," I said with a laugh. "This is too much."

"Not at all, Watson," answered Holmes. "Just look at how he stands and dresses, and how he carries himself. It is easy to see that this man was in the military and was an officer. As you know, many of our soldiers serve in India. His tanned skin suggests that he has recently returned from that country."

Mycroft continued. "He is still wearing his military boots. That tells me he didn't leave the army long ago."

"He doesn't walk like the soldiers I have seen who are in the cavalry and ride horses," added Holmes. "He wasn't in the Royal Engineers, either, as he is too heavy for the work they do. Yet he wore his hat to one side of his head. You can see that one side of his brow is less tanned than the other. That can only mean he was in the artillery."

"His clothes also show that he is in mourning," said Mycroft, "and has lost someone close to him. Since he is doing gift shopping for children, my guess is that he lost his wife. He carries a rattle for a very young child. And a picture book for an older child."

I saw that Holmes had been completely honest when he described his brother earlier.

"By the way, Sherlock," said Mycroft. "Would you be interested in hearing about a problem I have been asked to look into?"

"My dear brother," Holmes replied, "I would be delighted."

Mycroft Holmes rang the bell. He scribbled a note on a piece of paper, then handed it to a waiter.

"I have asked my neighbor to join us," he explained. "His name is Melas and he is Greek. He asked me to look into a matter that I will let him explain."

After a few minutes, Mr. Melas joined us and told his tale. "As you may already know, I make my living as a Greek interpreter. For example, when the hotels have Greek guests who don't speak English, they call me. Sometimes I am called at odd hours to help travelers who have just arrived in London. So I wasn't surprised when a Mr. Latimer called on me two nights ago. He said a Greek friend was visiting and that he needed my services. He seemed in a hurry and rushed me into a horse-drawn carriage.

"We hadn't gone far when Mr. Latimer did the most astonishing thing. He pulled a small club from his pocket and placed it on the seat beside him. Then he closed the windows of the cab. To my surprise, the windows were covered with paper. I couldn't see out.

"He then explained that he didn't want me to

know where we were going. He also told me that I must not go to the police and that I would be rewarded for my troubles. He was a large man, and there was nothing I could do.

"We drove for nearly two hours," Melas continued, "until the cab came to a stop. Mr. Latimer opened the door and I got out. We were at a house with an arched doorway. To either side was a yard with grass and trees. But other than that, I had no idea where I was.

"Inside, Mr. Latimer left me with an older, grim-looking man who wore glasses. This man also warned me to do as I was told, or else I would be in trouble. He explained that there was a Greek gentleman in the house. He wanted me to ask the man questions and translate the answers into English. The man in glasses made it very clear that I wasn't to say anything else to my fellow countryman.

"He took me into another room. It was large

and dimly lit. I could see expensive furniture and feel a thick, rich carpet under my feet. A suit of Japanese armor stood by a fireplace. The man with glasses told me to sit down. Just then, Mr. Latimer appeared with the Greek stranger. To my horror, this man's face was deadly pale. He looked very weak. As bad as he looked, I was more shocked to see that his face was covered with bandages. His mouth was hidden by a large piece of tape. Mr. Latimer pushed the man into another chair.

"The man with glasses then told me to ask a series of questions. The bandaged man answered each by writing on a piece of paper."

Mr. Melas continued his strange tale as Holmes, Mycroft, and I listened. "The first question was: Will you sign the papers? His answer was: Never! Then, he added: Only if I see her married by a Greek priest who I know.

"This continued for a while," Melas said.

"Then I had an idea. Once I was sure that Mr. Latimer and the other man could not speak a word of Greek, I began to add my own questions to theirs. That way, the Greek man and I were able to communicate without the others knowing. The conversation went something like this:

"'It is no good to resist. *Who are you?*'

"'I don't care. *I am a stranger in London.*'

"'You know what will happen to you, then? *How long have you been here?*'

"'Do what you must. *Three weeks.*'

"'The property can never be yours. *What is wrong with you?*'

"'As long as it does not go to you. *I have not eaten in days.*'

"'You will go free if you sign. *Where are we?*'

"'I will never sign. *I don't know.*'

"'You are only harming her. *What is your name?*'

"'Let me speak to her. *Kratides.*'

"'Sign, then you can see her. *Where are you from?*'

"'Then I shall never see her. *Athens.*'

"Just then, the door opened and a woman stepped into the room. She was tall, with black hair, and she wore a loose white gown. She came in asking for Mr. Latimer. But when she saw the bandaged man in the chair, she cried out his name, 'Paul!'

"Kratides tore the tape from his mouth and called to her. Her name was Sophy. He rushed into her arms, but Latimer quickly grabbed the woman and took her away. The other man did the same with Kratides. When the man with the glasses returned, he gave me money. Then, with a horrible laugh, he warned me not to speak to anyone about that night.

"Mr. Latimer returned and took me to the carriage. Again, we rode for hours with the windows closed. When the carriage finally stopped, I got out and saw that I was in the country. The carriage sped off, leaving me alone. From there, I made my way to the nearest town and caught the first train into the city.

"I do not know where I was," Melas said, "or who I was dealing with. I only know that I want to help that poor man. I told my story to your brother and to the police, and now I am telling you, Mr. Sherlock Holmes."

"And what have you done, Mycroft?" asked Holmes.

The older brother handed us a newspaper. He pointed to a notice that read:

A reward to anyone with information about a Greek gentleman named Paul Kratides from Athens, or a Greek woman named Sophy.

"That was in all the daily newspapers," explained Mycroft. "But there has been no answer."

"What about the Greek embassy?" asked my friend.

"Nothing," was the reply.

"Have you contacted the Athens police?" Holmes asked.

"This is why Sherlock is famous and not I," said Mycroft to me. "He has the energy to follow the trails, but I don't. If you would like to investigate the matter, Sherlock, then by all means . . ."

"Thank you, Mycroft," answered Holmes. "I will look into it. And I will keep you and Mr. Melas informed. In the meantime, Mr. Melas, I would be careful. By now, Mr. Latimer and his friend know you have not heeded their warnings. You may be in danger."

My companion and I left the Diogenes Club and headed toward Baker Street. We stopped at a telegraph office so that Holmes could send off several messages. Then, as we continued on our way, Holmes asked me what I thought of the case.

"It seems to me," I said, "that the Greek woman was kidnapped by Latimer. Perhaps from Athens."

"I disagree, Watson," said Holmes. "Latimer did not speak a word of Greek, so I don't think he was ever there. On the other hand, the lady spoke English. I believe she has been to England before and met Latimer on one of those visits. Perhaps they became romantically involved. She did not give Mr. Melas the impression that she was being held captive."

"I believe that she and Mr. Kratides are sister and brother," I continued. "It seems likely to me that she has some sort of fortune. Her brother has come to England to end the affair between his sister and Latimer. But Latimer and the other man will stop at nothing, and they have taken Kratides prisoner. She has only just found out by accidentally walking in on them. So now she is a prisoner, too."

"Excellent, Watson!" cried Holmes. "And it is up to us to stop their game. With any luck, we will receive an answer to the notice in the papers. After all, she was not in hiding before and probably knows people here. Then we may be able to find them all."

We reached Baker Street, made our way up the stairs, and opened the door to the flat. We were astonished to see Mycroft Holmes waiting for us. "Come in, gentlemen, come in," he said.

"How did you get here?" Holmes asked his brother.

"I passed you in a carriage," Mycroft answered. "We got an answer to our notice. It is from a Mr. J. Davenport. He says he knows Miss Kratides. And that she has been staying at The Myrtles, in Beckenham."

"Then that is where they all are," said Holmes. "We will call at Scotland Yard at once and bring Inspector Gregson with us."

"It would be wise to bring Mr. Melas, too," I added. "We may need an interpreter."

"Yes. Excellent, Watson," said Holmes. "Now let us find a carriage, quickly!"

As Mycroft and I headed down the stairs, I turned back and saw Holmes reach into a drawer. He pulled out a gun, put it in his pocket, and followed us to the street.

It was getting dark when we arrived at the home of the Greek interpreter. But we discovered that Mr. Melas was gone. His landlady explained that a man had come for him and that they had left together by carriage. She said the visitor was a short man, with glasses and an odd laugh.

From there, we rushed to Scotland Yard. Inspector Gregson joined us, and we made our way to the train station. It was ten thirty by the time we reached Beckenham. A carriage took us the rest of the way.

The Myrtles was a large, bleak house with a large yard. The windows were dark, and the place seemed empty.

"They are gone," observed Holmes as he examined the road leading to the house. "These tracks were made very recently. They were left by a carriage full of luggage and passengers."

There was no answer at the door, so Holmes forced open a window. Once inside, we saw that we were in the large room that Melas had described. The suit of Japanese armor stood by the fireplace. As we looked around, we heard a low moaning sound. It was coming from upstairs.

We bolted to the second floor and followed the sound to a room. The door was locked from the outside, but the key was still in the keyhole. Holmes opened the door and entered the room. In an instant, he was in the hallway again, coughing and clutching his throat.

"It is gas," he gasped. We looked in the room and saw a lamp of some kind. It burned with a small blue flame. It was the lamp that was giving off a poisonous gas. In its dim light, we saw two figures slumped in a corner. Holmes took a deep breath and went back into the room. He opened a window, grabbed the lamp, and threw it outside. Then we picked up the two men and dragged them into the hallway.

Their faces looked worn, and their lips were dry with thirst. Their hands and feet were tied together. One of the men was the Greek interpreter, Melas. The other had a pale face, covered with bandages. It could only have been Paul Kratides.

We were too late to save poor Mr. Kratides. But Melas recovered within the hour and explained what had happened. As we had guessed, the man with glasses had visited the Greek interpreter. Melas could do nothing but return to Beckenham, where he was forced to question Kratides again. Nothing could convince the brother to hand over his sister's fortune. So both men were locked in the deadly room while Latimer and his partner fled with Sophy Kratides.

❦

It was only later that Holmes and I uncovered all the details of the case. Mycroft's newspaper notice had been answered by a gentleman who had come to know Miss Kratides. He told us that she came from a wealthy Greek family. It was on a visit to England that she met Mr. Latimer. Miss Kratides' friends knew the Englishman was up to no good, and they sent word to her brother. But when he arrived in England, Latimer and his partner took the brother captive. Miss Kratides did not even know her brother was being kept in the same house. The bandages, we guessed, were to disguise him should his sister catch a glimpse of him by accident. As we know, it did not work.

Months after that, Holmes and I noticed a

curious story in the newspaper. It told how two Englishmen had met a tragic end while traveling in Hungary with a woman companion. The police decided that the two men had argued. And that during the argument, they both suffered deadly injuries. Holmes' only comment was that the police are sometimes wrong. And that he was sure the sister would tell a different story—one in which she had seen justice done.

The Adventure of the Six Napoleons

⌒

Inspector Lestrade of Scotland Yard sat quietly. He often visited Sherlock Holmes and me when we shared rooms on Baker Street. Holmes was always eager to find out what was going on at police headquarters. And the inspector welcomed any help that Holmes might provide.

"Are you working on anything interesting, Inspector?" asked Holmes.

"No, nothing much," Lestrade replied. "Well, perhaps there is something. But it may be a matter more for Dr. Watson than for you. I say that because it seems to be some form of madness I am dealing with. Why else would someone go out of his way to destroy images of the French Emperor Napoleon?"

"Oh, really," said Holmes, disappointed. He sat back in his chair.

"How else can you explain it?" asked Lestrade. "This person breaks into homes, doesn't steal anything, then smashes statues of Napoleon that he finds there."

"This becomes more interesting," Holmes said, sitting up again. "Please, continue."

"It all started four days ago," Lestrade began. "The first report came from a man named Morse Hudson. Mr. Hudson owns a small shop in the Kennington Road district where he sells paintings and small statues. It seems he and his assistant were in the back of the shop when they heard a loud crash. They rushed to the front of the shop to see what had happened and found a small plaster statue of Napoleon on the floor. It was smashed to pieces. But there was no one in the shop."

"Was it a statue?" asked Holmes. "Or was it a bust of just the head and shoulders?"

"It was a bust," answered the inspector. "Mr. Hudson then went outside. Onlookers had seen someone run from the shop, but the person was long gone. The piece didn't cost much at all. So there didn't seem to be any real harm done.

"But last night," Lestrade continued, "there was another report. A Dr. Barnicot lives just down the road from Mr. Hudson's shop. The doctor has a large collection of books, paintings, and other items about the French emperor. In fact, he bought two busts of Napoleon from Mr. Hudson's shop. He had one in his home. He put the other in his office in Lower Brixton.

"Well, this morning, someone broke into Dr. Barnicot's house. Strangely, nothing was stolen except the bust of Napoleon. It had been taken into the yard and smashed."

Holmes grew more interested. "Go on, Inspector," he said.

"It gets even stranger, gentlemen," said Lestrade. "This afternoon, Dr. Barnicot discovered that someone had broken into his office and destroyed his other Napoleon."

"Tell me, Inspector," Holmes said. "Were Dr. Barnicot's Napoleons exactly the same as Mr. Hudson's?"

"Yes, they were, Mr. Holmes," replied Lestrade.

"Then the man you are after is not driven by a hatred of Napoleon," said Holmes. "After all, there are thousands of images of the French Emperor in London. This man seems to be after identical Napoleons."

"Or perhaps," suggested Lestrade, "he lives nearby. Perhaps he is just starting his mad attacks and happened to find these three first. What do you think, Dr. Watson?"

"It's possible," I replied. "Perhaps he or someone in his family was injured or harmed in the great war. It's possible he blames Napoleon in some odd way."

"But I find it interesting," interrupted Holmes, "that the man took Dr. Barnicot's Napoleon outside. Would a madman think to break the bust outside where it would not disturb the family? Then, in the doctor's office, he broke it inside because he knew no one was around to be disturbed. No, we are not dealing with madness, gentlemen.

"And, I warn you," said Holmes sternly. "These events may seem harmless and insignificant. But it is hard to say that anything is unimportant. Remember, Watson, the dreadful case of the Abernetty family? It all began when I noticed how deep the parsley had sunk into the butter on a hot day. No, nothing is without meaning. And I would appreciate it if you would keep me informed, Inspector."

It wasn't long before we heard from Lestrade again. A message arrived from him the very next morning, asking us to come to 131 Pitt Street. Holmes and I rushed over as quickly as possible and saw a crowd gathered in front of the house. As we made our way through the onlookers, it was clear that the mystery had become more serious.

Lestrade was already inside. "Well, Mr. Holmes," he said. "It has turned to murder. This is Mr. Horace Harker. He is the owner of the house and is also a reporter for a newspaper. He will explain to you what he knows."

Harker sat in his dressing gown. His face showed that he was very upset. "All my life, I have been reporting other people's news. And now, here is the most amazing story in my life, right in my own home.

"Mr. Holmes, as a newsman, I often do my writing at night. And so, I was at work this morning at three, in my upstairs den. That's when I heard someone downstairs. I listened carefully, but the house had gone silent. Then, five minutes later, I heard a frightful scream. I rushed downstairs and found the window open. I saw that my bust of Napoleon was gone from the shelf above my fireplace. I have no idea why a thief would take that piece. I bought it four months ago from Harding Brothers on High Street. It is only made of plaster and isn't worth very much."

Harker took a deep breath and continued. "I went to the front door and opened it. It was there I saw the dead man, lying on the front steps. I called out for the police, who arrived at once."

"And the murdered man? Who was he?" asked Holmes.

"We don't know," answered Lestrade. "The body has been taken away, but I can tell you he was tall, dark, very strong, and around thirty years old. He was poorly dressed. There was a knife near the body, and we found this photograph in his pocket."

The photograph was a snapshot of a man. He was rough looking, with thick eyebrows and a large chin.

"And where is the bust?" asked Holmes.

"In the front garden of a nearby house," answered Lestrade. "We can go there now if you'd like."

We left Mr. Harker, who said he must still do his job and report the murder for his newspaper. We walked down the street and found the bust, which lay in pieces on the grass. Holmes picked up several bits of plaster and studied them closely.

"Well, we know that the man we are after brought the bust to this yard for a reason," he said. "It is an empty house, so he knew he would not be disturbed. But there is another empty building closer to Mr. Harker's home. Our man must have carried the Napoleon here because of this street lamp. He wanted privacy, but he also wanted to see what he was doing."

"Come to think of it," said Lestrade, "both of Dr. Barnicot's Napoleons were broken where there was light. But what does it mean, Mr. Holmes?"

"I'm not sure, Inspector," answered my friend. "That is for us to figure out."

"It seems to me," Lestrade said, "that the answers will come when we find the name of the murdered man."

"Then I will let you follow that line of inquiry,"

said Holmes. "Meanwhile, I will look for my answers elsewhere. By the way, Inspector, when you speak to Mr. Harker, please tell him that I believe we are dealing with a madman—one who is driven by anger at Napoleon. He will find that helpful for his article."

"You don't really believe that, do you, Mr. Holmes?" asked Lestrade.

"Perhaps not," said Holmes. "But the readers of Mr. Harker's newspaper will find it interesting. And now, we have work to do. I would like to keep the photograph that was found in the dead man's pocket, Inspector. And if you would meet Watson and me at Baker Street tonight at six o'clock, we can continue our investigations together."

Holmes and I left Pitt Street and made our way to Mr. Hudson's shop on Kennington Road, where the first Napoleon had been destroyed.

"Yes, I sold two Napoleon busts to Dr.

Barnicot," said the store owner in answer to our questions. "I bought all three of them from Gelder & Company, on Church Street. They make statues and other types of stonework."

"So the Napoleons went from Gelder & Company to this shop, then on to Dr. Barnicot's," said Holmes. He then showed Hudson the photograph and asked, "Do you know this man?"

"Why, yes," replied the shopkeeper. "His name is Beppo. He helped out in the store for a short time. But he quit last week and I haven't seen him since."

We thanked Mr. Hudson and left his shop. Our next stop was Gelder & Company. When we arrived, we saw a yard filled with sculptures and pieces of stone. Inside, about fifty men were hard at work.

Holmes and I found the manager and asked him about the Napoleons. He told us the three busts sold to Mr. Hudson had been from a batch of six. The other three had been sold to Harding Brothers on High Street.

He also explained how they were made. Plaster is poured into an empty mold, he said, like pouring mud into a bucket. Once the plaster dries, the mold is taken apart to reveal the finished bust. The manager told us the busts had been made in the room we were in. Then they were put in another room to dry.

When Holmes showed him the photograph, the manager became very angry. "Him!" he yelled. "Yes, I know him. His name is Beppo. He worked here over a year ago. But one day he got into trouble with the police. They chased him here, where they caught him and arrested him. He was put in jail, but I'm sure he's out by now. I think Beppo's cousin works here. We could ask him."

"No, no," cried Holmes. "Don't say a word to the cousin. It is very important we keep the matter a secret. But you can tell me something. When did you sell those six busts, and when was this man Beppo arrested?"

The manager looked in his record book and told us the six Napoleons had been sold on June 3 of last year. He said that Beppo had been arrested just before that, sometime around the end of May.

The trail was becoming warm. We now knew that Beppo had been arrested over a year ago. Shortly after his arrest, three Napoleons were sold to Mr. Hudson, and two of those had gone to Dr. Barnicot. The other three were sold to another shop, Harding Brothers on High Street. One of those went to Horace Harker. We also knew that Beppo had been released from jail recently, and went to work at Mr. Hudson's shop. It seemed clear that Beppo was the one hunting down the Napoleons.

After our visit to Gelder & Company, we

continued on the trail of the Napoleons. Our investigation led us to the Harding Brothers shop.

"Yes, we got the busts from Gelder & Company," Mr. Harding said. "One was sold to Mr. Horace Harker. The others were sold to a Mr. Josiah Brown and a Mr. Sandeford."

"I see," said Holmes. "And have you ever seen this man?" He handed Mr. Harding the photograph.

"No, I can't say that I have," replied Harding.

"Just one last question," said Holmes. "Is it possible for someone to look in your books and see to whom the busts were sold?"

"I suppose so," Harding answered. "I don't keep the books under lock and key."

Our questions answered, Holmes and I headed home to meet Lestrade. On the way, we picked up a newspaper. The headline read: "Murder by a Madman." The article was written by Horace Harker. In it, Mr. Harker had written that both the police and Sherlock Holmes thought there was only one explanation for the murder—that it had been committed by someone who was out of his mind.

The Inspector was already at Baker Street when we arrived. His day had been as productive as ours.

"That's right, gentlemen," said Lestrade, "I know the name of the dead man. One of the officers down at headquarters knew him. His name was Pietro Venucci and he was a member of a well-known and dangerous gang. I think the gang was after the man in the photograph for some reason. Venucci was carrying his photograph so he could find him and kill him.

"I believe," Lestrade continued, "that Venucci followed his intended victim, saw him enter Harker's house, and then waited outside. When he came out, the two fought. But it was Venucci who was killed. How is that, Mr. Holmes?" said Lestrade with a big smile.

"Excellent, Lestrade!" cried Holmes. "But what about the broken busts?"

"Are you still concerned about the busts?" asked Lestrade. "Really, Mr. Holmes. I'm quite sure I need only question the other members of Venucci's gang. They will lead me to the man in the photograph."

"I disagree," said Holmes. "Instead of chasing after Venucci's gang, I believe we will find our man elsewhere. There are two busts left from the original batch of six. One has been sold to Mr. Josiah Brown. The other to a Mr. Sandeford. We will find our man at the homes of one of these two gentlemen. And since Mr. Brown lives closer, my guess is we'll have better luck there.

"Inspector, please stay for dinner," said

Holmes. "Afterward, we will all pay an evening visit to Mr. Brown. Watson, would you please ring for a messenger? I have a very important letter to send . . ."

We left Baker Street at eleven o'clock that night and were soon at the home of Josiah Brown. The house was dark, and I was glad Holmes had asked me to bring along my gun. It looked as if everyone had gone to bed. A single lamp shone over a side door and cast a circle of light on the garden path. The rest of the yard was dark, and we waited outside in the shadow of a fence.

We didn't have to wait long. As my companions and I crouched in the darkness, someone opened the gate and quietly rushed up the garden path. Then he disappeared in the shadows by the house. After what seemed like many minutes, we heard a faint creaking noise. It was the sound of a window being opened. Moments later, the light of a lantern flashed inside the house.

The stranger must have found what he was looking for, because he reappeared outside on the garden path. In the dim light, I could see that he was carrying something under his arm. He crouched down and placed the object on the ground. This was followed by the sound of breaking plaster. At that moment, Holmes rushed from the shadows and tackled the stranger. Lestrade and I followed, and the burglar was quickly in handcuffs. We turned his face to the light, and saw that it was the man in the photograph.

The Inspector and I carefully watched our prisoner. Meanwhile, Holmes crouched on the garden path. He was looking at the bust of Napoleon, shattered into a hundred pieces. He picked up piece after piece and held each one up in the light. Just then, the front door of the house opened and a man appeared.

Holmes looked up and said, "Mr. Josiah Brown, I presume?"

"Yes," the man replied. "And you must be Sherlock Holmes. I received your letter by messenger this evening and did exactly as you asked. I locked every door, turned off all the lights, and made sure my family was upstairs. I'm glad to see you caught your man."

Lestrade stepped forward and said, "Yes, and now I'll take him down to the station. I'm very grateful to you, Mr. Holmes, for bringing this affair to an end."

"On the contrary, Lestrade," said Holmes. "The end hasn't been written yet. If you would care to visit Dr. Watson and me tomorrow evening at six o'clock, I shall be able to give you the complete story."

When we met the next evening, Lestrade told us what he had learned about the burglar. His name was indeed Beppo. He had been a skilled sculptor in the past, but had turned to crime in recent years. The captured man probably made the six Napoleons himself, while he worked at Gelder & Company. But he would not explain why he was now destroying them.

Holmes seemed bored and impatient as he listened to the Inspector. Then the bell rang, announcing a visitor. Our landlady, Mrs. Hudson, let the visitor in, and he joined us in the parlor. He was an elderly man, with bushy sideburns. He was carrying a large bag, which he placed on the table.

"Mr. Sherlock Holmes?" the man asked.

"You must be Mr. Sandeford," Holmes replied.

"Yes," said our visitor. "I received your message and came at once. But I don't understand how you knew that I owned a bust of Napoleon. Nor why you want to buy it from me. You do know that I didn't pay very much for it?"

"Yes, Mr. Sandeford," said Holmes. "I understand. But I wish to own it and I am willing to pay the amount stated in my message."

Our visitor shrugged his shoulders and opened the bag. He reached in, removed a sixth bust of Napoleon, and placed it on the table. Here, finally, was the object we had only seen before in pieces.

Holmes paid Mr. Sandeford and thanked him. When our puzzled visitor was gone, Lestrade and I watched Holmes in amazement. He spread a large cloth over our table and placed the bust on it. Next, he took the metal poker from the fireplace and struck the bust, breaking it into pieces. Holmes sifted through the pile of rubble, then picked up a single piece. He held it up for us to see. A small, round, dark object poked out from the white plaster.

"Gentlemen," he cried, "I give you the Black Pearl of the Borgias!" Lestrade and I stared in stunned silence. Then we both began to clap wildly as if we had just witnessed a great stage performance. Holmes' cheeks grew red, showing an emotion that one rarely saw in him.

"This valuable beauty belongs to the Prince of Colonna," he explained. "I first heard of it over a year ago, when it went missing from the Prince's room at the Dacre Hotel. I was not able to help the police in finding the pearl or the thief. But we suspected the Princess' maid, a woman named Lucretia Venucci. I have no doubt that it was her brother Pietro who was murdered the other night. And it would not surprise me if she knew our friend Beppo as well."

"But if the pearl was stolen by the maid," I asked, "how did it get into this Napoleon?"

"Allow me to retrace the steps, starting with

the theft over a year ago," replied Holmes. "The maid took the pearl. She gave it to her brother and Beppo for safekeeping and to sell. Then, for some reason, Beppo was pursued by the police. He had the pearl on him and ran to Gelder & Company. With the police closing in, he saw the batch of six Napoleons drying in the factory. He took one of the busts, carved a small hole in the soft plaster, and placed the pearl inside. Then he covered up his handiwork with more plaster. He was arrested by the police, but the pearl was safely hidden.

"While Beppo served his year in jail, the six busts were sold. Three went to Morse Hudson's shop. Two of those were sold to Dr. Barnicot. Three others went to Harding Brothers, where they were sold to Horace Harker, Josiah Brown, and Mr. Sandeford.

"Then our friend was released from prison. His cousin still worked at Gelder & Company, and it was he who found out where the Napoleons went. Beppo managed to get a job at Morse Hudson's shop, where he smashed the first bust to see if it contained the pearl. It didn't. So he found both of Dr. Barnicot's pieces and broke them, too.

"He still didn't find the pearl," Holmes said, "so he traced the other Napoleons to Harding Brothers. He looked in their books and saw that one of the busts had been sold to Horace Harker. It is at Mr. Harker's that he met his old partner Venucci."

"But why did he kill Venucci?" asked the Inspector. "And why would Venucci have a picture of Beppo? He already knew what he looked like."

"I'm not sure why Venucci was killed," said Holmes. "Perhaps Beppo stole the pearl from Venucci. Perhaps they were partners, but Venucci blamed the other for losing the pearl. As for the

photograph, Venucci probably used it to search for Beppo. He may have shown it to people and asked them if they had seen the man.

"It's not important," continued Holmes. "What is important is that I knew he would not stop until he found the pearl. I had Mr. Harker report that we were dealing with a madman. I counted on Beppo reading the newspaper. That way, he would think that it was safe for him to seek out the last two busts.

"Mr. Brown's home was the closest, so I sent him a message. I told him to turn out all the lights and make sure everyone was safely upstairs. When we found our man but not the pearl, I knew right away that the treasure could only be in the very last Napoleon—the one belonging to Mr. Sandeford. I sent him a message, asking him to come to Baker Street. The rest you know.

"And that," concluded Holmes, "is how the pearl made its way from the Dacre Hotel to my hand." He held up the precious pearl for all to admire.

"Remarkable, Mr. Holmes, absolutely remarkable!" exclaimed Lestrade. "I've worked with you on many cases before. But I can't remember a single one that makes me more proud to know you."

"Thank you, Lestrade. Thank you," said Holmes. "If another little problem comes your way, do let me know. I would be happy to give you a hint or two as to its solution."

What Do *You* Think?

Questions for Discussion.

c๏

Have you ever been around a toddler who keeps asking the question "Why?" Does your teacher call on you in class with questions from your homework? Do your parents ask you questions at the dinner table about your day? We are always surrounded by questions that need a specific response. But is it possible to have a question with no right answer?

The following questions are about the book you just read. But this is not a quiz! They are designed to help you look at the people, places, and events in the story from different angles. These questions do not have specific answers. Instead, they might make you think of the story in a completely new way.

Think carefully about each question and enjoy discovering more about this classic story.

1. Sherlock Holmes had extraordinary skill in examining details and events to solve cases. How well do you observe details and analyze events to come to your own conclusions? Did it become easier to solve the cases with each story you read?

2. Did you solve any of the mysteries before Holmes? Which ones?

3. Why does Watson tell the stories instead of Holmes? What are the advantages and disadvantages of this? Who would you prefer to tell the stories?

4. Holmes is a man who never seems to let anything slip past him. In "A Scandal in Bohemia," he obviously underestimated Irene Adler. Why

might this have happened? Have you ever underestimate an opponent?

5. Holmes tells Watson, "You see, but you do not observe." What do you suppose he means by this? Do you see or observe?

6. How does Holmes compare to other detectives you have read about or seen on television?

7. Holmes believed that when all the impossible elements of a crime had been ruled out, whatever was left, even if it seemed unlikely, would lead you to the truth. What incidents or events in the book are good examples of this? Have you found this to be true in your own life?

8. In "The Adventure of the Speckled Band," what were some of the suspicious clues found in the bedroom? Did you recognize these as clues? Were there any false clues that led you to a different solution?

9. Doctors are said to make good criminals. Do you agree with this statement? Why or why not?

10. Many of Holmes's decisions are not quite in accordance with the law. For example, in "The Blue Carbuncle," Holmes allows the criminal to go free. Can you think of any other times when Holmes does what he wants rather than what the law requires? How do you feel about his actions? What would you do in his place?

Afterword

by Arthur Pober, EdD

⟳

First impressions are important.

Whether we are meeting new people, going to new places, or picking up a book unknown to us, first impressions count for a lot. They can lead to warm, lasting memories or can make us shy away from any future encounters.

Can you recall your own first impressions and earliest memories of reading the classics?

Do you remember wading through pages and pages of text to prepare for an exam? Or were you the child who hid under the blanket to read with a flashlight, joining forces with Robin Hood to save Maid Marian? Do you remember only how long it took you to read a lengthy novel such as *Little Women*? Or did you become best friends with the March sisters?

Even for a gifted young reader, getting through long chapters with dense language can easily become overwhelming and can obscure the richness of the story and its characters. Reading an abridged, newly crafted version of a classic novel can be the gentle introduction a child needs to explore the characters and story line without the frustration of difficult vocabulary and complex themes.

Reading an abridged version of a classic novel gives the young reader a sense of independence and the satisfaction of finishing a "grown-up" book. And when a child is engaged with and inspired by a classic story, the tone is set for further exploration of the story's themes, characters, history, and details. As a child's reading skills advance, the desire to tackle the original, unabridged version of the story will naturally emerge.

If made accessible to young readers, these stories can become invaluable tools for understanding themselves in the context of their families and social environments. This is why the Classic Starts series includes questions that stimulate discussion regarding the impact and social relevance of the characters and stories today. These questions can foster lively conversations between children and their parents or teachers. When we look at the issues, values, and standards of past times in terms of how we live now, we can appreciate literature's classic tales in a very personal and engaging way.

Share your love of reading the classics with a young child, and introduce an imaginary world real enough to last a lifetime.

Dr. Arthur Pober, EdD

Dr. Arthur Pober has spent more than twenty years in the fields of early-childhood and gifted education. He is the former principal of one of the world's oldest laboratory schools for gifted youngsters, Hunter College Elementary School, and former director of Magnet Schools for the Gifted and Talented for more than 25,000 youngsters in New York City.

Dr. Pober is a recognized authority in the areas of media and child protection and is currently the U.S. representative to the European Institute for the Media and European Advertising Standards Alliance.